You Can Do It Tom Mouse!

by Dicky Barr
& Joanna Scott

Tom Mouse loves his grandad. Grandad Mouse
was a great explorer when he was young.

Tom wants to be a great explorer too.

Grandad Mouse gives Tom a present,
a globe of the world.

Tom spins the globe, and where it stops
is where he will go.

When the globe stops, Tom is pointing at the highest mountain in the world.

"I am going to climb Mount Everest!" he says.

At times, Tom
was not sure he
could manage
the challenges
that he took on,

but Grandad Mouse
always said,

"You can do it
Tom Mouse!"

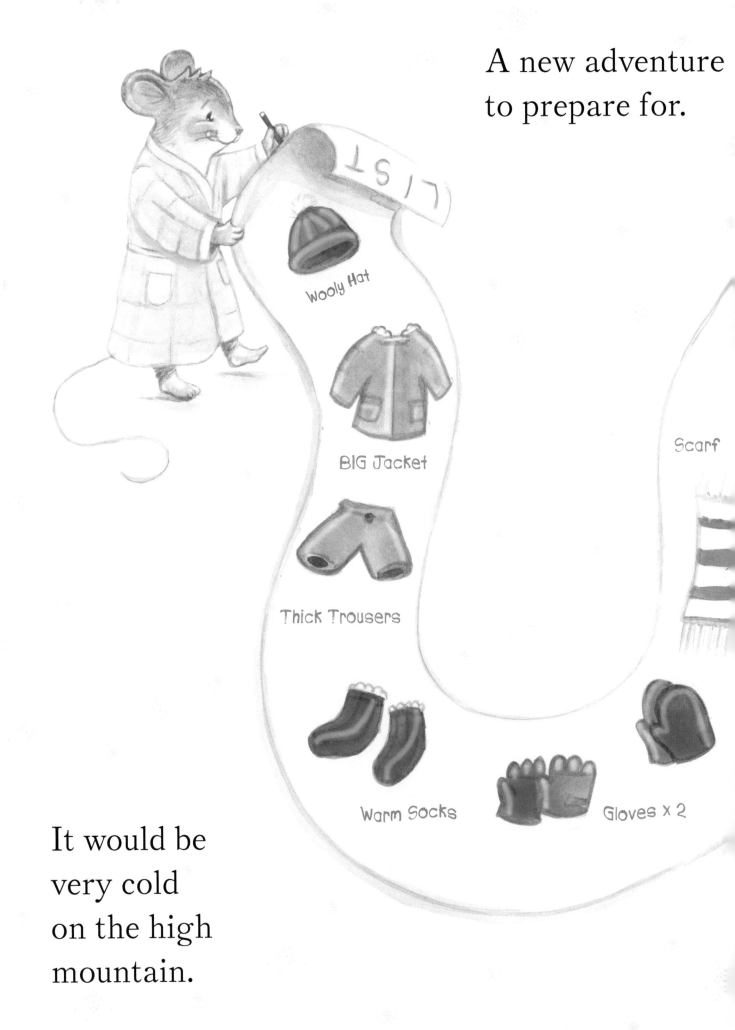

A new adventure
to prepare for.

LIST

Wooly Hat

BIG Jacket

Thick Trousers

Scarf

Warm Socks

Gloves x 2

It would be
very cold
on the high
mountain.

Tom made a long list of all the clothes
he wanted to take with him.

Cheese
Biscuits

Spiky Boots

Goggles

Camera

Ice Lollies

Matches

He wondered what
else he would need.

The list went on and on...

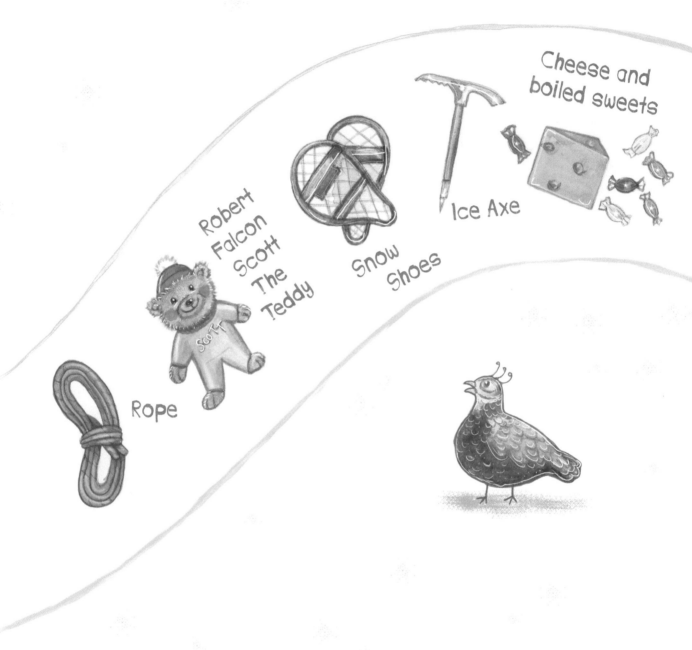

Rope

Robert
Falcon
Scott
The
Teddy

Scott

Snow
Shoes

Ice Axe

Cheese and
boiled sweets

and on...

and ON!!

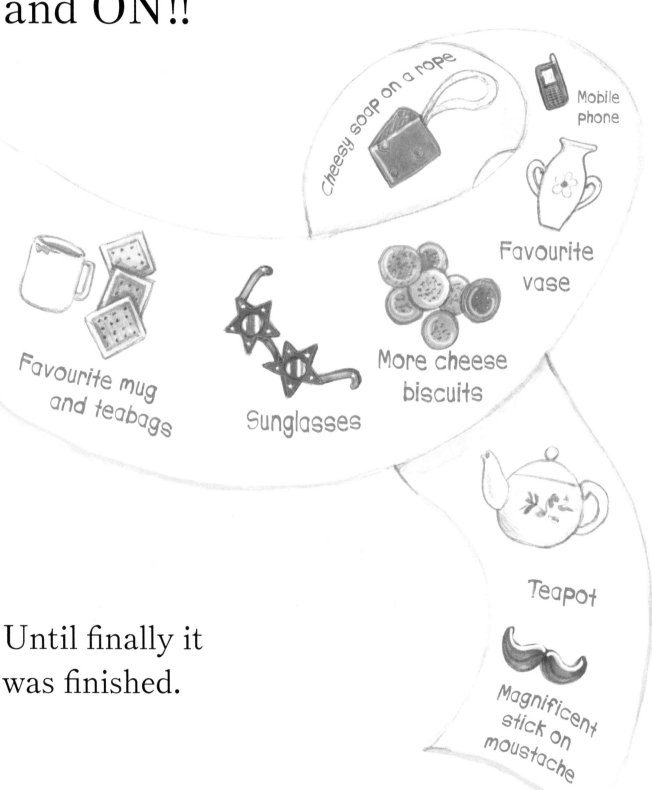

Cheesy soap on a rope

Mobile phone

Favourite vase

Favourite mug and teabags

Sunglasses

More cheese biscuits

Teapot

Magnificent stick on moustache

Until finally it was finished.

So, with help
from Grandad
Mouse, Tom
was ready
to go...

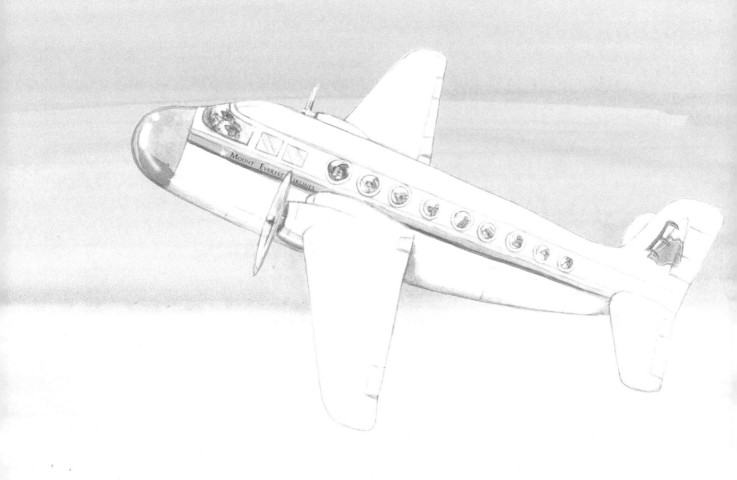

"GOOD LUCK!"

"You can do it
Tom Mouse!", says
Grandad Mouse.

Tom finally arrives!
"Wow, Mount
    Everest is

    SO BIG"

says Tom.

"How am I going to carry all of my bags through this deep snow?"
Suddenly Tom hears:

CLUMP!

CLUMP!

CLUMP!

and he turns around to see...

"Hi, I'm Simon, the marathon-running yak."

"I'll carry your bags for you Tom Mouse. It's only 100,000 steps to Everest Base Camp."

"Thank you", says Tom.

"Why do you have that bell around your neck Simon?", asks Tom.

"Because my horns don't work!", says Simon.

And they both laugh.

Simon is super speedy and they arrive
at Base Camp in no time at all.

After sharing cheese and biscuits
for breakfast

Tom waves goodbye to Simon and
starts his climb up Mount Everest.

At a very deep icy valley...

"I can't reach across to the other side", says Tom.

Then he hears:

CRUNCH!

CRUNCH!

CRUNCH!

in the snow and he
spins around to see...

"Hi, I'm Dawa,
the snowboarding
snow leopard."

"I'll get you across the gap."

"Hang on!"

"Ready for take-off?"

"Go!" says Dawa.

And they fly across the gap.

"WHEEEEE!"

shouts Tom.

"Thank you Dawa", says Tom, as they share some cheese and biscuits.

"Why do you like snowboarding, Dawa?"

"Because it keeps me so cool!", says Dawa.

And they both laugh.

Tom carries on with his climb, until he comes to a huge wall of ice.

"How am I going to climb this last piece of slippery ice?", asks Tom.

Then he hears...

DUMDEE DOO!

DUMDEE DOO!

DUMDEE DOO!

and he turns around to see...

"Hi, I'm Helen the
disco dancing yeti."

"I'll help you to get
on top of the ice!"

"I'm a yeti
and I always
leave a big
impression."

And they both laugh!

Helen pogos up and down. Tom stretches as high as he can.

"I CAN'T REACH"

says Tom.

POGO

POGO

POGO

POGO

But then, he thinks of Grandad Mouse saying,

"YOU CAN DO IT TOM MOUSE!"

...so Tom makes one final

S-T-R-E-T-C-H

and...

He makes it!

A little bit further and
Tom will be at the top
of the mountain.

"I Did It!"

shouts Tom.

"Thank you to all my friends!", and he waves to his new friends and thinks about his Grandad too.

Tom Mouse is at the top of Mount Everest. He is the highest mouse in the world!

"I knew you could do it!"

Grandad Mouse is so proud of Tom.

Tom Mouse gazes at his wonderful globe, and says,

"I wonder where my next fantastic adventure will be?"

How many Himalayan monal
birds did you see in the book?

Lightning Source UK Ltd.
Milton Keynes UK
UKHW051558100919
349488UK00009B/140/P